GET A GRIP

ALYSON SHELTON

WEST 44 BOOKS™

Please visit our website, www.west44books.com.
For a free color catalog of all our high-quality books, call toll free 1-800-398-2504.

Cataloging-in-Publication Data
Names: Shelton, Alyson.
Title: Get a grip / Alyson Shelton.
Description: Buffalo, NY : West 44, 2027. | Series: West 44 YA verse
Identifiers: ISBN 9781978598560 (pbk.) | ISBN 9781978598553 (library bound) | ISBN 9781978598577 (ebook)
Subjects: LCSH: Siblings--Death--Fiction. | Interpersonal relations--Fiction. | Gymnastics--Fiction. | Families--Fiction. | Friendship--Fiction.
Classification: LCC PZ7.1.S545 Ge 2027 | DDC [F]--dc23

First Edition

Published in 2027 by
Enslow Publishing
2544 Clinton Street
Buffalo, NY 14224

Editor: Caitie McAneney
Designer: Tanya Dellaccio Keeney

Photo Credits: Cover (background) andreiuc88/Shutterstock.com; cover (gymnast) Real Sports Photos/Shutterstock.com.

Printed in the United States of America

CPSIA compliance information: Batch #CS27W44: For further information contact Enslow Publishing LLC at 1-800-398-2504.

For my brother, Michael.
And for anyone grieving, you are not alone.

SUMMER
1984

I KNOW, I KNOW

Get a grip already!

Jenny says.
My best friend shakes
her sun-kissed blond hair
and laughs.

I *know*
I'm talking too much again.
About gymnastics.
About how much I love it.
About how I want to be an Olympian
just like Mary Lou Retton.

Mary Lou is strong.
So powerful—
and everyone seems to love her.

I want to be
just
like
her.

I'M STRONG

And short.
(My brother Todd
calls me stocky,
a word I *hate*.)
With long brown hair
that is impossible to braid.

My other brother Michael tells me,

You're just right.
I love you.

You're not supposed to have favorites,
but I do.

They are off camping together.
Brothers, but also friends.
I don't know how Michael does it,
put up with Todd.

He's a better sibling than I will ever be.

NOW I'M LAUGHING

Jenny and I lie in front of the TV.
The avocado-green shag carpet
scratches my belly.

My mom sits behind us
on the blue vinyl couch.

Jenny is talking about boys.
Boys pay *a lot* of attention to her.
She's bubbly,
beautiful, confident.
All the things I'm not.

Ryan is her latest crush.
His dark brown eyes are
majestic.
His curly hair is
perfection.
And his smile is
magnificent.

But what about his personality?

Jenny just rolls her eyes.

MARY LOU MIGHT WIN!

My mom loves gymnastics because
she loves me.

Before I was born,
she was a super-glam stewardess.
She's still pretty to me, even though
Todd calls her *chunky*.

She knows Mary Lou
would be the first American woman to
win the all-around:
every gymnastics event.

When Mary Lou gets her second
perfect 10,
we jump up
and down screaming.

I know it's not cool to
love your mom,
but I do.

I CAN'T SLEEP

I'm way too excited.
Mary Lou won the gold!

I lie under my
lavender eyelet bedspread
and vibrate with excitement.

I want to talk all night
with someone who cares like I do.

Problem is,
I don't know anyone.

Maybe I'll meet a friend
who is just as *obsessed*
with gymnastics
at my new gym.

It's the gym the *Olympic* coach runs,
after all.

I start there in three weeks!

THE PHONE RINGS

It's late at night.
Past midnight
and I'm still awake,
struggling to find sleep.

I jump out of bed
and run down the hall
to my parents' room.

I'm scared.
Nothing good happens this late.

MY MOM PACES

back and forth between
their king-size bed
and the never-used fireplace.

Todd, Todd, slow down.
I can't understand what you're saying.

She listens to Todd.
And Dad and I listen to her breathing.
And the moments that pass

feel like forever.

SHE GRIPS THE PHONE

He might still be alive.

My dad and I lock eyes.

We don't say Michael's name.
But it is there,
in the air between us.

Unsaid.

MICHAEL IS MISSING

My mom tells us,

He felt sick from the altitude and
told Todd he'd meet him
back at the car.
But Todd couldn't find
him anywhere.

Tomorrow, they'll
send out a search party.

He's still alive.
Pray, think of him,
imagine him safe.

In the morning,
they will find him.

I don't say the only thing I can think:

But what if they don't?

I TRY TO THINK POSITIVELY

To imagine Michael on a bed
of pine needles.
Staring at the star-filled sky,
knowing in his heart that he will be
found in the morning.

Alive.

I TELL HIM I LOVE HIM

I love you,
I whisper.
Please don't die,
I beg.

The tears run down my face,
soaking my pillow.

I so want to believe he's OK.

But I feel like he's already left me.

THE SUNLIGHT WAKES ME

I must have slept after all.
But not much.
My eyes feel itchy.
Like they have sand in them.

I lie in bed
and try to stop the only thought
in my brain from forming.

But I can't.

I just have a feeling.

I know he's gone.

MY MOM STANDS UP

from the dining table
to give me a hug.
She holds me so tight,
I can barely breathe.

Have they called?
I wonder out loud.

My dad—trim with military-like neatness
even in times like these—
finally speaks,
No, not yet.

My mom whispers,
almost to herself,

There's still hope.

THE PHONE RINGS

and we all jump.

My father answers it this time.

Hello? Good morning, Sheriff.
Yes, yes, I'm sure you did.
Yes, thank you.

He hangs up the phone and tells us,

They found his body.

Michael is dead.

I HOWL

Like an injured animal.
Like I've lost my other half.

Because that's the truth.

I'll never be the same person without Michael.

I don't even know
who I am now.

IT'S ALL A BLUR

Todd comes home.
People send flowers.
I cry.
There is a funeral.
Or memorial.
Or a service.
I don't know the right word.

I don't know the right anything.

I don't feel right,
not anymore.

AT THE SERVICE

People say too many things.

He was only your half brother.

At least you have another brother.

Be strong for your parents.

God doesn't give you any more
than you can handle.

I wish they would say:

I'm sorry this happened to you.

This is the worst thing.

I NEVER THOUGHT ABOUT HALVES

until today.

Michael was my brother.
Period.

When Todd teased me.
Or our dad ignored me.
He'd let me sit with him
on his always-unmade bed.

We'd watch a baseball game.
He'd push his wavy black hair
back from his hazel eyes.
Push his glasses up his nose, and
teach me how to keep score.

He'd make me laugh.
He never cared that I was a girl
or too young.

He made me feel safe.

THE REC CENTER

It's my last gymnastics
practice here.

After five years at the center,
this is it.

It's hard to believe.

I try to act
like I always do.
But I feel all the girls
looking at me and whispering.

About my dead brother or
the fact that I'm leaving—
or both.

I practice my skills.
Run drills.
Help set up and
break down equipment.

I don't even cry
when I say goodbye.

I'm ready
to leave.

JENNY AND I HAVE PLANS

We made them last week, before . . .
before everything.

And my mom thinks I should go
to the beach.
Usually my second favorite place
after the gym.

It'd be good for you.
Give you something fun to do.

So I put on my bikini.
I grab my towel.
I get in the car.

And pretend all of this is normal.

JENNY IS ALREADY THERE

She lifts her hand to wave to me.
Next to her, there's Ryan.
Next to him, some other boy.
I can't remember his name.

Brandon? Jeremy? John?

They grin.

How's it going?
Pretty day, right?

I don't say,
My brother has been dead for a week.

I say,
Yep, great day for the beach.

And ignore my stomach flipping
from anxiety.
I sit down next to
what's-his-name
in the blindingly bright sunshine
and try not to frown
too much.

HIS NAME IS BRANDON

He's cute. Tall. Athletic.
Probably out of my league.

I'm "stocky."
And sad.

Hey, I'm Kelly.

We stare at the seemingly
endless ocean.

I don't know what to say.

Jenny elbows Ryan.
She's worried I'm gonna blow it.
I can feel them waiting for me
to make it less awkward.

I don't.

JENNY TAKES CHARGE

Standing, pulling off her enormous
FRANKIE SAY RELAX T-shirt.

It's like she's talking to me
without saying a word.

I remember all our years
at the beach together.
There's a script for this.
She's giving me my next line.

So I stand up and shout,
Race you!

And I know I've said the
exact right thing
by the way Jenny smiles
and starts sprinting
toward the shore.

I PLUNGE IN

I run so fast,
beating everyone,
as usual.
I hit the water and
fall forward with a splash.

Laughing.

I dive under the water.
And feel a wave crash above me.

I'm in my happy place
with my best friend
and a cute boy.

FOR A MOMENT

I forget
that my brother is dead.

I am bobbing out in the ocean,
treading water.

I'm smiling at Brandon.

Then he asks me a question,

So what did you do this summer?

And I remember Michael.
And I don't know how to answer.

How am I supposed to answer?

JENNY ANSWERS FOR ME

She doesn't mention Michael.
And I don't either.

Kelly was totally obsessed
with the Olympics.
Kelly's like, a rad gymnast.
Didn't you know?

Brandon looks at me,
almost like he's seeing me
for the first time, and says,

Oh, yeah? That's cool!
I love the Olympics.

Brandon asks,

So what's your favorite event?

I stumble over my words,

Um, vault.

NO BOY HAS EVER CARED

about gymnastics.
Or what I think of it.
Usually they just
change the subject.

Why am I not more excited?

I also like floor a lot.

I give up trying
to act normal,
and I dive
deep, deep underwater,
just so I can be alone.

MY MOM IS COOKING

I see her in the kitchen when I come in
through the sliding glass door.

Her back is to me, but I know her
movements as well as my own.
Putting noodles in boiling water,
browning ground beef to blend with the
Ragú spaghetti sauce.

Her hands and thoughts are busy
with the routine.

And then, suddenly, she stops.

I REALIZE SHE'S CRYING

silently.
Her back is still to me.
And her hands are on her face.

I know I should comfort her.
That's my job.
I am the only one in this family
who understands her feelings.

AND I TAKE THAT SERIOUSLY

Mom? Are you OK?

She turns to me,
wiping tears from her eyes.
She tries to smile,
to spare me.

But I know what she's feeling
because I feel it too.

Michael is dead.
And nothing feels the way it did.

I HUG HER

And she cries harder than before.

They keep calling me his
"stepmother."
His real mom died
when he was a baby.
I adopted him when
he was so young.

He was my son.
Our son.

And now he's gone.

Her body sags with grief.
And even though we are
the same height,

I am so strong that
I keep her upright.

WE EAT DINNER TOGETHER

The four of us.
My mom.
My dad.
My brother
(half brother?) Todd.
And me.

Todd is handsome.
Polo shirts and
pressed khakis.
Think Alex P. Keaton
from *Family Ties*
but with an edge.

He knows how to get what he wants,
except when it comes to me.

I'm a constant disappointment.

TODD IS MUCH OLDER

I'm 15 and he's 27.
He never lets me forget
how much more he knows than me.
(Even though he's still living
at home because his girlfriend Tracy
dumped him.)

My mom glances across
our polished dining room table
at his dinner.

He's barely touched it.

Todd pushes his plate away.

My mom asks,

Aren't you hungry?

HE GETS UP

He says,
I'm meeting the boys for sushi.

Without taking his plate
to the kitchen or
saying thank you.
Without a thought for us.

And it ticks me off.

Aren't you going to say thank you?

I say before he's gone.

HE TURNS AROUND

I can tell he's angry.
He spits his words at me.

Oh, excuuuse me.
Of course, Princess Kelly.
What am I saying
thank you for exactly?

I try to stay calm when I say,

For the dinner Mom made.

He doesn't try to stay calm
when he says,

She's not my mother.

My mom looks like he slapped her.

Our dad,
who is Alex P. Keaton
with no edge,
just sits there,
twirling spaghetti on his fork.

WE STARE AT DAD

I know he can feel our eyes on him,
willing him to say something.

I barely even realize
I'm speaking out loud.

Say something,

I whisper.

And then I say louder,
almost begging,

Dad, say something.

HAVE FUN WITH YOUR FRIENDS

he tells Todd.

The grin that spreads across
Todd's face
makes me want to
punch him.

Quiet tears pool in Mom's eyes.

Before they fall, she turns away
and heads into the kitchen.

I hear her turn the water on.
And the clatter of the dishes
as she begins to scrape
and rinse them.

I WANT TO SCREAM

Instead, I make fists,
digging my nails into
the palms of my hands.

Todd chuckles to himself.
I ask him,

What's so funny?

He says,
You wouldn't understand.

But I want to know.
What is it?

Dad drinks his soda,
the ice cubes clinking in
his glass.

I ask Todd,
Is it about Michael?

AND HE SNAPS

Get real.
Not everything is about Michael.

But I don't
understand.

Why *isn't* everything about him?
Or why isn't *something* about him?

He's dead.

Why don't we talk about it?

I EXPLODE

Why not?

Todd and Dad say nothing.
They don't even look at me.

He just died.
He's never coming back.
Can't we at least talk about him!?

Dad stays silent.

Todd says,

What is there to say?
He's gone.
End of story.

MY FACE IS WET WITH TEARS

I don't know when I started crying.
I wipe my cheeks.

Todd and Dad look at me
like I'm crazy.

Why aren't you crying?
Why aren't you sad?

Todd spits out his words,

Looks like you're sad enough for all of us.

AS TODD TURNS TO GO

I ask,

Why do you hate me?

Finally, Dad speaks up.

That's enough, Kelly,
Todd has to go.

Todd checks his image in the mirror,
pops his collar,
and turns to me.

His voice low, he says,

I know Michael and you
were real close.
And I know you wish I'd died
instead of him.
But could you be a little less
obvious about it?

FINALLY, I'M SPEECHLESS

I feel like I'm standing in a long tunnel.

All alone.

I hear everything,
but from a great distance.

The slam of the door
when Todd leaves.

The squeak of Dad's chair
when he pushes back from the table.

The loud grumble of Mom
running the garbage disposal.

THE PHONE'S RING IS MUTED

I feel like I'm in
the *Peanuts*.

I know my mom is talking to me.
Trying to hand me
the phone.

But her words are impossible
to make out.

I crumple into the chair.

MOM LOOKS SO WORRIED

Kelly! Are you OK?

I take a deep breath
and suddenly,
I'm back.

I'm OK, Mom.
Don't worry.
I was just feeling weird.

My mom grabs me
and hugs me.
So tight.
She's crushing my ribs a little.

But I don't say a word.

MY MOM SAYS

I'm sorry.
I'm sorry.

I don't know what she's apologizing for.

It's OK, Mom.
Everything is going to be OK.

She nods,
but I'm not sure
if she believes me.

I don't even
believe myself.

MOM INSISTS

You should call Jenny back.
She's the one who called just now.

But I don't feel like talking
to Jenny.

Go ahead. You don't have
to sit here with me.

I know my mom is
trying to be nice.

She always thinks she
knows what's best for me
and tries to help.

But right now,
I wish she'd stop pushing me
to have fun.

SHE WATCHES ME

until I walk into the kitchen
to call Jenny back.

I punch in her number.
The one
I’ve had memorized since
second grade.

844-6883

My finger pauses.
It doesn’t press 3.

I don’t finish the call.

Instead I wrap the phone cord
around my finger and
yell out to my mom,

It’s busy!

JENNY HAS CALL WAITING

So her line is *never* busy.

Mom sits on our couch
and pats the spot next to her.

Uh-oh.
I sit down.

Kelly, did you call Jenny just now?

How does she know?
What is she,
some kind of mind reader?

I stay silent.

Kelly, I don't think you
called Jenny.

I don't know for certain why,
but I can guess.

You're having a hard time.
So much change.

And I'm just not sure you're
ready for more.

HUH?

Where is she headed with this?

I don't ask out loud.
I just wonder.

And then she says,

I know you're very excited
to start at this new gym.
And we're so excited for you.

But maybe now isn't the time?

WHAT?!

I stand up
shaking my head.

I've worked for a spot
in this gym
for *years*.

All the hours of training . . .

I snap, *No.*

I am starting at the new gym.

It's the one thing.
The ONE thing
I have in
my life to look forward to.
And there is no way
you are going to take that
away from me.

And then I stomp up to my room
and slam my door.

SOUTHERN CALIFORNIA GYMNASTICS ACADEMY

That's the name of the gym.
My new gym.
But everyone calls it

THE Academy.

Because it's famous.

The head coach
is also the Olympic coach.

And girls from all over
Southern California train here.

We have to drive almost an hour
each way to get there.
But I know it's worth it.

I'M NERVOUS WALKING IN

I'm wearing my favorite leotard.
It's a boatneck tank top with
pink neon stripes.

I wish my hair was French braided.
But my mom and I don't know how.

And neither of us can seem to learn.
There's probably a book somewhere,
but that's *so* not gonna happen.

So I make do with a ponytail.

THE GYM IS HUGE

From the outside, it’s pretty blah.
But on the inside,

OH MY GOD.

There are more balance beams than
I can count.

Maybe 20?

Two full floors.
Two!
We didn’t even have one
at my old gym.

Just crummy old mats we’d unfold
before practice and
fold back up after.

THE FLOOR SPRINGS SQUEAK

as a gymnast
runs across the floor and into
a roundoff
back handspring
double twist.

Wow.

She gets so much air.
Her form is incredible.
And she almost sticks the landing.

Coach Gary pats her on the back.

Nice, Angie!

But she doesn't even crack a smile.
Just gets back in line,
ready to go again.

MY BRIEF TOUR IS OVER

It’s time for me to join
the other girls.

But I need another minute.
I remember the water fountain.

I’m going to get a quick drink.

I sip the cool water.
Give myself a
silent pep talk.

This is all you’ve ever wanted.
You can do this, Kelly.

I'M GOING TO MAKE THE COMPETITION TEAM

I tell myself as I step onto the floor.

All the new girls gather around
to stretch and warm up
and listen to
to Coach Gary's speech.

Welcome to Southern California
Gymnastics Academy.
The best gym
on the West Coast.

We are not like your old gym.
Every girl here is talented and
wants to make the team.

You are going to have to dig deep.
Not once in a while.

Every day.

AND HE MEANS IT

I'm working on my middle splits
when Coach Carol comes by.
She pushes me down
until I can feel red-hot pain
moving up my inner thighs.

How's this?
she asks.

This might be my first day here.
But I already know the answer.

It's good.

WE FINISH STRETCHING

and they sort us into
four groups.
One for each event.

The four gymnastics events are:

Vault = The best!
Uneven Bars = Fine.
Balance Beam = Love it—NOT.
Floor = Rad!

My group goes
to vault first.

YES!!!

TEN GIRLS PER GROUP

I look around.
Of course, I don't know anyone.

Not really.

Just Angie, the girl from before.
I try to get ready.

I tell myself,
Focus on the vault, Kelly.

We're starting with a
front handspring.

Just to get used
to the equipment.
Easy.

I've done this vault
hundreds of times.

Just relax.

MY FEET POUND DOWN

the runway and I hit
the springboard
perfectly.

My hands touch the vault,
propelling me up and over.

I love this feeling.

Almost flying.

I know I'm too old for my
Wonder Woman Underoos.
But I still like to imagine
I'm unstoppable like her.

That I'm capable of
amazing feats.

I RUN BACK TO MY PLACE IN LINE

I've already learned,
there is no walking in this gym.

While I wait for my turn,
I watch Angie vault.

I'm trying hard
not to be jealous.

The girl next to me,
Iliana,
says quietly to herself,

Incredible.

And she is.

BUT BEFORE I CAN DECIDE

if Angie is
my main competition
or my enemy,
she lines up behind me.

She shyly smiles.
Says,

Hey, I'm Angie.
Nice vault.

Inside, my heart leaps.

She liked my vault!

But I try to stay cool.

Yeah, you too.
I'm Kelly.

AND JUST LIKE THAT

three hours pass.
Three hours of
vaults and
floor routines.
Practicing beam
and bar dismounts.

Of chalking up
and stolen giggles.
Of comparing hand tears
and taping up to prevent more.

Of Angie showing me the way,
trading Olympic facts and our
dreams for the team.
Of wondering how
I got so lucky.

WE HIGH FIVE

She says,
See you tomorrow!

when we part
ways on the sidewalk
outside the gym.

Can't wait!
I say.

And I can't.

For three hours,
I chased my dreams.

I felt 15
years old.

For three hours,
I didn't think about Michael.

I didn't even know
that was possible.

I JUMP IN OUR CAR

a baby blue Toyota Camry
with baby blue interior.

Looks like you made a friend,
my mom says.

Yeah, I think I did!
I spill, excitedly.
Her name is Angie.
She's really nice.

We talked about Mary Lou
and Team USA,
and I think she knows
more than I do!

About everything.

She didn't tease me at all,
not even once.

THE PHONE IS ALREADY RINGING

when we get home.

I run up to my room
to answer it.

It's Jenny.
She talks about Ryan.

A lot.

But it's OK.

I'm writing our names
with flowers and hearts
on my goofy paper bag
book covers.
And I know she's doing
the same at her house.

It almost feels
like old times.

JENNY ASKS

You want to hang out this weekend?

And instead of saying no.

Or using my six-hour practice
on Saturday as an excuse.

I surprise myself and say,

Sure. That would be fun.

SHE MUST BE SURPRISED TOO

because she pauses a second
before she asks,

Can Ryan and Brandon come too?

I say,

Yeah, why not?

I can hear Jenny jumping around
her room as she hollers.

This is gonna be rad!

And then I find myself smiling again.

THE REST OF THE WEEK

is a dream.

Every day, practice.

I'm strong in the gym,
full of power,
always pushing myself
to go harder.

And—my new friend, Angie?
She's close to perfect.
Makes everything look effortless.

And she doesn't put people down,
not ever. The only other
person I've known like that
was Michael.

Sometimes I struggle
with the right words
when I'm with friends.

With Angie,
it feels different.
Like we share more
than *just* gymnastics.
We share the way
we see the world.

We can be silly too.
We say corny things like,

You stuck it! (the landing, that is)
That was a perfect ten!

MY OTHER FRIENDS

School starts and I have even less time
to hang out with my other friends.

Gymnastics always comes first,
but I try to squeeze in time with
Jenny, Ryan, and Brandon.

Brandon is
definitely out of my league,
but he doesn't seem to know it.

We all go jogging together.

To help with my training.

Brandon tells me,

I cannot believe
you've already
worked out for six hours!
You're . . . phenomenal.

AND I THINK

he actually means it.

That I'm *phenomenal*.

Most of the time, boys
make fun of me for
being so strong.

But not Brandon.

In moments like these,
I can't believe this
is my life.

I'm smiling.
I have friends.

I might even have a boyfriend?

AND THEN I REMEMBER MICHAEL

And I find time to cry—
usually in the shower,
where no one can hear me.

I'm still not "over it."

I don't know what to do
with "it."

The sadness.

I miss Michael.

His birthday is coming up.
He would have been 25.

I'M STABBING CARROTS

with my fork.

I want to say something.

Todd and Dad are talking
about baseball.

Michael's favorite sport.
Michael's passion.

He loved baseball the way
I love gymnastics.

He wasn't a great player,
but he was *obsessed* with stats.

HE'D WATCH ONE GAME

on his portable
black-and-white TV
and listen to
another on the radio.

We'd sit on his bed
together.

I loved listening to the
scratch of his pencil
and the patter of the sportscaster.

SMELLING HIS OLD SPICE

aftershave and feeling the warm
sunlight through the blinds.

It's the best memory.

I can't stay there
for a long time though.

It makes me too sad.

The fact we'll never
have a moment
like that again.

TODD NOTICES ME

Kelly, are you crying?
What the heck?

Oh no,
I stayed in that sad place
too long.

I feel my cheeks go red.

Finally I say,

It's nothing.

Todd says,
Wow, you're crazy.
You know that?

I do feel crazy sometimes.

I wonder why I
still miss Michael so much
when no one else
seems to care.

I TRY TO EXPLAIN

It's almost his birthday.
I'm just thinking how . . .
how he'll never be
twenty-five.

My dad says nothing.
My mom looks like
she's about to cry now.

And Todd is angry
with me.
Again.

Now, you've made
everyone *sad, Kelly.*
Why do you have
to ruin a nice dinner
with all your drama?

I DON'T KNOW

I'm happy one minute.
And then,
the next,
I'm crying.

Michael has been
dead for two months.

I don't know how
it's been that long.

I don't know how
I have
a new friend,
a new gym,
my first boyfriend
(maybe),
and Michael will never know
any of it.

BRRINNNNNG

Saved by the phone.

I wipe tears
from my face
and run to the kitchen.
Hoping that it's Jenny
or Angie.
Anyone to take me
away from this.

Hello?
Abbott Residence.

Hey! Jenny says.

Phew.
I set the phone on the counter
and run upstairs to my room,

yelling over my shoulder.

Hang up the phone for me,
please!

I GRAB MY PHONE

Covering the handset,
I holler,

I'm on!

I wait to hear the click
of the phone being
hung up downstairs.

Instead, Todd gets on.

Hey, Jenny,
How's high school?
Breaking all the boys' hearts?

I roll my eyes. Ew.
I want to scream.
But Jenny only giggles.

Like I said,
Todd is handsome and
charming.

To other people.

THE PHONE *FINALLY* CLICKS

Jenny says
Byeeeeeeeeeeeeeee.
For a grody amount
of time, even though
there's no way
in the world
Todd
could hear her.

Let's have a sleepover
at your house!
This weekend!

She hasn't wanted to
sleep over here in ages.

She knows how early
I go to bed
and wake up
to practice.

AND NOW SHE CAN'T WAIT

Please!
You can even invite Angie!
I want to meet her!
It'll be fun.
Come on!

Once Jenny decides on
something,
anything,
it's almost impossible
to say no.

I've never learned how to
say no to Jenny.

So I say,

Chill—I'll ask!

Yesss!!!
she squeals in victory.

MY MOM IS SITTING

on her bed, staring into space.

Is it OK if I have a
sleepover on Saturday
with Jenny and maybe Angie?

    She lights up.
    That's such a great idea!
    I'd love to have the
    girls over.
    Like old times.

Yeah,
like old times.

JENNY IS STOKED

Awesome!

I'm . . .
I'm . . .
I don't know.

It feels weird
to be excited.
Feels weird to think
of my friends meeting.

Call Angie!
Then call me back.

I have homework . . .

Totally, do that too.

And then she giggles
and hangs up.

I sit on my bed
and stare into space.

ANOTHER DAY AT THE GYM

I chalk up my hands.

Dip them in the bin
and clap off the residue.
It makes a tiny white poof
in the air.

I love the routine,
now that I know it.

Angie and I exchange small smiles.

Iliana cracks a joke.

We laugh hard and
work harder.

We point our toes.
Stick our landings.

We all strive to be perfect.

AFTER PRACTICE ON SATURDAY

Angie rides home with me.
Rattling off the latest news
about Team USA.

And then it hits me.
I don't want Angie and Jenny to meet.
Let alone have a sleepover.

Jenny is my best friend,
but she can stress me out.
To the max.

And who knows what she'll say?
About me or Michael.

I hate that
I say
yes

when sometimes
I want to say
no.

SLEEPOVER DINNER

My mom makes crunchy tacos.

It's fun.
She calls it a
taco bar.

There's little bowls with different toppings.

Olives.
Tomatoes.
Cheese.
Lettuce.

And crunchy shells.
And ground beef.

Jenny gushes,

Mrs. Abbott, these tacos are like
totally scrumpdillyicious.
Like, completely
awesome.

Is it just me,
or is she being totally
over-the-top?

Angie just smiles
and takes another taco.

LATER, IN MY ROOM

We can't figure out
what to do next.

Angie and I are tired
from the long practice day.
Jenny is bouncing with energy.

I suggest renting a movie.
My mom could take us
to the video store.

Angie says,
Sure. Have you seen
WarGames*?*
I want to see that.

Jenny exclaims,
What about Flashdance*?!*

Angie stays silent.

But I know Angie well enough
to know that her mom
wouldn't want her watching that.

JENNY ASKS

How about Truth or Dare?

And I immediately want to yell

NO!

Why does Jenny
always have to do this?

Always have to
push people to do things
that might be uncomfortable?

Angie looks over at me.
Her eyes
silently pleading.

And I know I need to
do something or
this is going to get
super awkward.

MY SOLUTION

Ice cream.

Let's go to Thirty-One Flavors!
I know your favorite
is Quarterback Crunch, Jenny.

What's yours, Angie?
Mine is Pralines 'n Cream.

I hope if I talk fast enough
for long enough,
Jenny will forget
her original question.

I know we're not supposed to eat
so many sweets,
but it's Saturday!
And it's a sleepover!
Let's go!

OUTNUMBERED

Angie looks relieved.
She stands up and says,

Mine Is Jamoca Almond Fudge.

And Jenny must know
she's outnumbered.

Because as we leave my room,
Jenny looks
down the hall,
at Todd's closed door.

We should ask Todd if he wants to come.

Jenny is on her way to Todd's door
before I have a chance to stop her.

WHAT IS JENNY DOING?

Knock, Knock!
she sings.

I don't even know if Todd's home.
God, I *so* hope he's not.

I grab Jenny's hand.

Come on, let's go!
Ice cream won't wait forever.

Jenny stands her ground.

Chill, Kelly, chill.

JENNY KNOCKS AGAIN

Angie, trust me.
Kelly's brother is a total babe,
you want to meet him.

Angie says nothing and
my eyes are begging
Jenny to shut up.

It's not working.

Isn't he, Kelly?
Come on,
back me up.

I shrug.
He's my brother.

Jenny's cheeks redden.
Then she rolls her eyes and says,
Omigod, you're so weird about
brothers now.
It's kind of crazy.

I DROP JENNY'S HAND

And I snap.

I'm getting ice cream now.
If you want to wait around
for Todd like some
little puppy dog,
even though you already
have a boyfriend,
be my guest.

I can't believe I just said that.
But Jenny is really ticking me off.

She stares me down.
As I walk away, she says,

Just 'cause your brother died,
doesn't mean you get
a free pass
to be a total buzzkill
forever.

I KEEP WALKING

I don't even know what I would say
to her right now if I stopped.

I hear Angie's footsteps
on the stairs behind me.

When I get to the bottom of the
stairs, I run to the patio.

I want to escape.
But I don't know how.

THIS IS MY LIFE

Kelly, Wait!

Angie is trying to catch up with me.

I know she cares about me.
I feel it at the gym every day.

I want to talk to her about all of this.
I trust her.
But I'm afraid I'm going to cry.
Or say something mean.

I STOP

and Angie stands there,
searching for words.

I didn't know your brother died.
I'm sorry.

I sniff.
Thanks.

I feel like I should say something else.

I always feel like
I should comfort other people.
Even though I'm the one
who is grieving.

It's OK, I guess.

Why did I say that?
It's a total lie.
I'm not OK.

ANGIE FLINCHES LIKE I HURT HER

But it's not like *her* brother died.

And then my mom appears out of nowhere.
And Jenny comes down the stairs.

And the silence is so heavy
I can't take it.

I know I need to keep up appearances
for my mom.

Show her I'm "getting over it."
That I'm so happy
with my friends
and this sleepover.

So I blurt out,

Mom, will you take us to get ice cream?

She grabs her keys
and says, *My treat!*

SORRY

At the ice cream shop,
Jenny and I take turns
not looking at one another.

I know she wants me to apologize.

But I am *always* the one saying sorry.

And I'm not sorry.

Jenny hurt my feelings.
Again.

And if her feelings are hurt,
good.

I turn toward Angie,
and ask how she likes
her flavor.

JENNY DOESN'T CALL ME

the next two nights.
And I don't call her either.

The rest of the sleepover
was gnarly.
And not in a good way.

She kept giving me super
meaningful looks.
Saying things like,

Is there anything you'd like to say?

I WOULDN'T APOLOGIZE THEN

and I won't apologize now.
I have loads of homework
to do anyways.

Gymnastics really cuts into
my homework time.

Todd leans into my room,
What's up, loser?

I stare back at him.

He thinks he's so funny.

I can't believe Jenny thinks he's cute.

Gag me.

TOMORROW WE FIND OUT

who makes the competition team.
There are 40 girls
and 5 spots.

It's super intense!

Angie and I still smile and
line up near each other.
But things feel different
since the sleepover.

I don't know what will
happen if she makes the team
and I don't.

Will we still be friends?

MICHAEL'S BIRTHDAY

is this week too.
And I want to do something.
Remember him in some way.

But how?

Nobody wants to talk about him,
let alone honor
the day he was born.

I FEEL LIKE SO MANY THOUGHTS

are bouncing around in my head.
And I don't know where to put them.

So I just need to focus on

my split leaps on the beam,
my landing on vault,
my release move on the bars

If I focus on making the team.
then things will
work out with Angie.
We'll go back to how it was.

And Jenny, I don't know.

BUT THE LIST IS UP

And my name is not at the top.

My eyes sting,
and I can barely
catch my breath.

Coach Gary says,

There are so many talented girls.
It was such a difficult decision.

As you all know, there are
only five team spots.

We've selected four of those girls.

Chrissie T.
Lara
Iliana
Angie

And for the last spot . . .

MY HEART RACES

—we've selected four finalists:

Michelle K.
Katrina
Joanna
Kelly

We've never done this before.
But we feel like these four
girls need a little more time
to show us what they're made of.

And for the next six practices,
all the coaches' eyes will be on them.

EYES ON ME

Coach says,
Now let's get to work.
State is less than
four months away.
And it's ours to lose.

New Team.
New Groups.
New Life.

Angie is grouped with the team.
And I'm with the finalists.

I wish being a finalist
didn't feel so awful.

I WANT TO CRY

I'm heartbroken.
But I can't let anyone see.

The four of us:
Michelle K.
Katrina
Joanna
me.

We can't show weakness.

For the next six practices,
we must master each event.

ALL-AROUND PERFECTION

That's the goal.

We start with beam.
My worst event.
Sometimes I fall off—
a huge point deduction.

Michelle K. never falls off.
Her toes are perfectly pointed.

I make myself stop
staring at her.

I work on my dismount,
two back handsprings
into full twist,
instead.

PRACTICE GOES FINE

I'm not the best of the four of us.
But I'm not the worst.

I'm feeling extra weird
because today,
I thought I would know
if I made the team or not.

Instead I'm in this gross
in-between place.

The not-good-enough place.

AFTER PRACTICE

we're grabbing our stuff
and Angie and I bump into each other.

I'm so jealous of her
and her spot on the team.

Her whole life, really.
No dead brother.
Gymnastics perfection.

But I know good sportsmanship
is part of being on a team.

And that being a poor loser is bad.

So I say,

Congrats on making the team, Angie.

SHE SMILES

Thank you, Kelly.
Congrats on being a finalist.

She doesn't say,
I know you'll make the team.
She doesn't even say,
I hope you make the team.

Just,
Congrats on being a loser.

I WANT TO ASK

Do you think I'll make it?

But I'm afraid of looking as
desperate and sad as
I feel.

So I say,

Must feel good to make the team.

Angie looks surprised.
And again,
a little hurt.

SUDDENLY, I FEEL TEARS

in my eyes.
I grab my bag and run out.

Angie doesn't say anything.
She doesn't follow me.

She must think I'm pathetic.

LUCKILY, MY MOM

is waiting in her car by the curb.
I jump in and hope no one has
seen me acting like a big baby.

My mom glances over, and gasps,

Oh, Kelly, are you OK?

She reaches out for me.
And I pull away.

People are coming out of the gym.
We have to go before someone
sees me.

Mom, just drive.

She looks over at me again.
And then, *finally*, we leave.

ONCE WE HIT THE FREEWAY

I start to sob.
There's no one here
to hold it against me.

Kelly, what happened?

I can barely speak.
That's how hard I'm crying.

It's embarrassing.
I feel like I should be
grown up by now.

How am I still sobbing like a baby?

GET A GRIP

I think.

Kelly, please talk to me,
says Mom.

I wipe tears from my eyes
with the heel of my hand.

I pull up my T-shirt to dry my face.

I TRY TO CALM MYSELF

Then I say,
I didn't make the team.

My speech is still stuttering
from all the crying, but
I get it out.

That's OK, Kelly.
Gymnastics isn't
that important.
It's something you love,
but it's not everything.

I want to yell,

What do you mean?
It *is* everything!
It's the only thing that
makes any sense!
And I need to be
PERFECT.

BUT I DON'T SAY ANYTHING

I don't yell at all.

I swallow.
I dry my face.

I tell her about being a finalist.

She pats my hand.

We pretend like everything is fine.

WE EAT DINNER IN SILENCE

The three of us.
Mom, Dad, and me.

I don’t know where Todd is.
And I don’t really care.

The phone doesn’t ring.
Jenny is still mad at me.
And I’m not going to be
the one to apologize.
Not this time.

Angie won’t call.

Maybe no one will ever again.

AFTER DINNER

I go to my room and
try to do homework.
But I can't concentrate.

I wish I could draw.

I see people doodling in
their notebooks. But
all I can draw is
stupid girly stuff
like rainbows and flowers.

And I still suck at it.

The one thing I'm actually
great at—gymnastics—
it takes a whole gym.
And coaches and equipment.

I wish cartwheels and
handstands still made me
happy like they did
when I was five.

WHAT DO PEOPLE DO

when they have no friends?
When the brother they love
is gone?

I sit there, at my desk,
and stare at the wall.

And sob some more.

And then I take a bath
and soak 'til my skin
gets wrinkly like a prune.

Then I go to bed,
without talking to anyone
or doing my homework.

I really am a loser.

I'M STANDING AT MY LOCKER

staring into it like it holds
the answers to the universe.

Usually Jenny would be here.
We would chat and joke,
and walk to class together.

Instead, I'm doing my new thing.
Being a lonely, pathetic dweeb.

So I'm surprised when I feel
a gentle tap on my shoulder.

I turn to see Brandon, smiling.

Hey, what's up, Kelly?

I SMILE

I know it would
be negative amounts
of chill if I actually told
him what was up.
So I stick with,

Not much.
What's up with you?

He flips his hair back from his eyes.

Not much . . .
Well, wanna hang out sometime?

Huh.

I've been so caught up in
the hellacious drama that
is my life,
I'd totally forgotten about Brandon.

AND HOW CUTE HE IS

Totally,
I say.

I have practice every weeknight.
It's like,
pretty intense right now.
How about this weekend?

He nods.
That would be rad.

We walk to class and
he asks,

Did you find out about the team?

And he looks genuinely interested,
so I tell him as much
as I can in
three minutes.

And he listens.

He's throwing me a life raft,
and he doesn't even know it.

THE UNEVEN BARS STARE ME DOWN

I spit on my grips
and chalk up.

Gotta get the balance just right
for optimal stickiness.

I can't fall off the bars.
Not now.

I clap the extra chalk off.
Imagine I can ace this.

I START MY ROUTINE

Salto forward onto the high bar.
I nail my giants.
Legs straight and glued together,
toes pointed.

I pirouette my hands.
Changing positions without pause.

My rhythm is good
leading into my dismount.

I hit my full twist layout.
And I stick the landing.

Yes!

I salute the coaches.

And keep my smile to myself.
No need to rub it in anyone's face.

But I know, in my gut,
that I was awesome.

ANOTHER SILENT DINNER

I imagine Michael
cracking jokes and
keeping us laughing.

He never minded making
the joke about himself
if it made people happy.

Sometimes taking the risk
is worth it, right?

That's what I'm thinking
when I ask my mom,

How was your day?

I'M SO RELIEVED

when
my mom replies,

It was . . . good.
I did the shopping.
And played tennis with
Diane and Joyce.
We won.

My dad says nothing,
kind of stares into space.

I say,

That's nice, Mom.

We sound like
robots.

Talking about nothing.
Sticking to a script.

I WILL MYSELF

to be brave.

I ask,

What's your favorite memory of Michael?

My mom smiles.
She's quiet for a minute.
Tears fill her eyes,
but they don't fall.

You know how he struggled
with hitting the baseball
before he got glasses?

I nod and look at my dad.

HE'S NODDING TOO

My mom says,
When he hit that first ball
after he got his glasses.
The smile on his face.
It was pure joy.

My dad smiles and says,

I was so proud of him.

We all look at each other.
And there's a moment.
It's almost like Michael
is there with us.

Grateful to be remembered.

AND THEN THE MOMENT IS RUINED

Todd barges in.

I've got big news!
Drumroll, please!

He drums on the table,
since no one else is going
to be a total dipwad
and do that.

I'm engaged!

My mom and dad jump up.
My mom hugs him.

> *Oh my goodness!*
> *Congratulations!*

My dad pats him on the back.

> *You sly fox!*
> *Who's the lucky gal?*

It's Tracy!
We got back together
and now we're making it official.

MY DAD CHUCKLES

I haven't seen him
this happy for a long time.

This is wonderful!
I knew you had it in you
to settle down!

He keeps smiling and
congratulating Todd.

I tell Todd,

Way to go.

And head upstairs.

I hear Dad still asking questions,

When's the wedding?
When do we get to congratulate
the blushing bride?

I know it's immature to say
but . . .
gag me with a spoon.

I STARE AT MY PRINCESS PHONE

debating about whether I should
call Jenny
or Angie
or even Brandon.

My brother Todd—
my only (living) brother—
just got engaged.

Shouldn't I be feeling something?
Something other than
disappointment.

We were *finally* talking about Michael.

I swear I could feel him there.

And now I'm pretty sure
we'll never talk about him again.

TODAY, AFTER PRACTICE

we find out who
makes the team.

And I'm going into
this day with a
winning attitude.

I've worked my butt off
inside and outside of practice.

I'm good enough.

But I know being on a
winning team
is more than that.

And I know,
there is one more thing
I need to do.

BEFORE PRACTICE

I walk right up to Angie.

I decide not to waste any time.

I'm sorry, I say.
I was jealous you made the team.

She shifts on her feet
and looks down.
Then meets my eyes.

I continue,
And I felt weird about the sleepover.
I'm sorry I didn't tell you
about my brother.
But I didn't know how.
I liked being just Kelly here.
I liked forgetting.
And I don't know if that
makes me a bad sister.
I'm afraid it does,
but it's the truth.

I'm really sorry,
Angie.

ANGIE SMILES A LITTLE

and says.

I'm sorry too.

I can't imagine what
she has to be sorry for.

She tells me,

I totally wigged out.
Not because you didn't
tell me about your brother.
But because . . .

My dad died when I was twelve.
And I hadn't told you.
I haven't told anyone here.
I still don't know how to talk about it.
Not really.

Angie looks like she's about to cry.

WE HUG EACH OTHER TIGHT

I think we're both crying a little.

But that's OK, right?

We're both sad.
I don't think we should
be embarrassed about it.

But when we pull back
from our hug,
we both look down at
our feet
while we wipe our eyes.

ANGIE WHISPERS

Sometimes I write to him.
To my dad.
To tell him I miss him.
Or to let him know how I'm doing.

It helps.
It helps me feel like he's still here.

ANGIE SQUEEZES MY HAND

I think you're gonna make it,
she says quietly.

I don't know if she means
she thinks I'm going to
make the team.
Or make it through this.

I don't ask
what exactly she means.

It's just nice knowing
I have a friend like Angie.

Who understands why I'm sad.
And doesn't hold it against me.

THE PRACTICE IS A BLUR

Of routines
and salutes and smiles.

Of pointed toes
and stuck landings.

Of chalked up grips
and effortless splits.

Of double twists
and full giants.

Of sweat
and tightly braided hair.

Of girls who want this more than anything—
the ones who will get it
and the ones who won't.

GO CHANGE, GIRLS

We'll have the list up in
ten minutes.

Those 10 minutes
stretch out and feel
like an hour.

I'm so happy Angie and I
are friends again.

She sits with me
even as the girls go to
check the list.

Even though I'm
so nervous,
I feel safe with Angie.

She seems to understand,
without asking, that
I'm not ready.

That I have to sit here a
minute longer,
believing I made it.

IT'S ILIANA

who comes back to the locker room.

Are you going to look, Kelly?

I'm not sure what to say.
I'm worried that I will
fall apart if I don't make it.

And I know I can't say that
out loud.

SO I SHRUG

Iliana says,
I can tell you
if you want to know.
Or you can go look.
It's up to you.

Iliana is a good teammate
and leader.
She looks after everyone.
She cares.

I try to read her face for clues.
Is she smiling?

I want to believe she's smiling.

I STAND UP

and go to look at the list.

Angie and Iliana follow behind me.
Most of the girls have left.
But the remaining ones watch me.

I try to fix my face with a smile.
I want to be OK either way.
I want to be a good teammate.

I look.

Chrissie T.
Lara
Iliana
Angie
Kelly

I MADE THE TEAM!

Tears start to stream down my face.
Angie hugs me.
Iliana hugs me.

My other teammates,
Chrissie and Lara
hug me.

We’re all hugging each other.

They say,

Congratulations, Kelly!
You made it!
We’re so glad you’re on the team!

I can barely believe it.
I really am a part of something.
I made it.

OH MY GOD!

I can't believe it!
I'm so happy!

And I am.

I hug each member
of the team individually.

I hug Angie last.
We stand there for a minute.

And it hits me.
I don't think I could have
done this without her.

She helped me every step of the way.
Out of kindness.
Out of friendship.

Wow.

FOR THE FIRST TIME

in a long time,
I feel truly happy.

I made the team.
I have a great friend.

I tell Angie,

Thank you.
For being an awesome friend.
For always being kind.
For just being you.

Angie smiles and throws her arm
around my shoulder.

Of course!

We walk out of the gym.
I am almost skipping with happiness.

FOR DESSERT WE CELEBRATE

with ice cream.
My favorite.

I tell them the story
of making the team
and Todd actually listens.

And then I went and looked at
this list and my name was on it!
I couldn't believe it!

Dad barely touches his ice cream.
But he does say,
I'm proud of you, Kelly.

Mom hugs me and tells me,
I'm so happy for you, Kelly.
You worked so hard.

And Todd shakes his head and says,
Not such a loser after all, kid.

I WISH MICHAEL WAS HERE

But I don't say anything.

I take their compliments.
I try to feel all the
goodness around me.
Instead of what is missing.

It's hard.

But just when I'm starting to feel
overwhelmed, I remember what
Angie said
about writing to her dad.

And I think,
it's worth a shot.

THEN I HEAD UP TO MY ROOM

to do homework.

I unpack my social studies
and math books
covered in grocery bags.

We're required to do it each year.
Cut grocery bags and wrap
them around our textbooks.

I don't know what good they do.

But we make the best of it,
Jenny and I,
drawing all over them.
And writing messages to each other.

I SEE JENNY'S WRITING

BFFs Jenny + Kelly!
Love you girl!

on the back of my geometry book
and I realize how much I miss her.

I kept thinking she would apologize.

That our friendship meant more to her
than winning the argument.

I should call her.
She's been my best friend forever.
But what if that's not true anymore?

I PULL OUT MY TRAPPER KEEPER

and find an empty notebook page.
I prop my geometry book open
and start working on a proof.

Geometry is my worst subject.
And I'm having such a
hard time concentrating.

I look over at my dresser,
at my dust-covered
Def Leppard
and Mötley Crüe cassettes
and wonder,
how did I ever think
that was *the best* music?

I GUESS SOMETIMES WE CHANGE

and we don't even notice
that it's happening.

I wonder if
I'm changing so much
that Jenny and I can't really
be friends anymore?

I want to think about
that problem even less than
I want to do geometry.

I pick up my pencil,
grab a piece of
Bubble Yum bubble gum,
and get to work.

BUT THE THOUGHT KEEPS NAGGING ME

The thought that I need to tell
someone else
my news.

And just because I don't want to apologize,
doesn't mean I don't want to talk
to Jenny.

I do.

The phone rings six times.
Maybe she's not going to pick up.
But then she does.

Hello?

Hi. It's me . . . Kelly.

Oh, hey.

There's something I wanted to tell you.

Oh yeah, what?

IT BUBBLES UP LIKE SODA

I made the team.

Oh my god, Kelly, that's so rad!
Congrats!

Thank you,
I say,
feeling the smile
on my face.

LESS THAN PERFECT

I know our friendship isn't perfect.
Jenny doesn't understand me
the way Angie does.

About gymnastics,
about loss.

I want Jenny to apologize,
to understand how she hurt me.

But maybe first
I need to get honest
with her.

I PAUSE, THEN SAY IT

Jenny, you really hurt my feelings.

And then I wait, scared,
but proud of myself.

> She pauses,
> and I'm sure she's hung up.
> Then I hear,
> *I'm sorry.*

Really?

> *I feel like you're so into gymnastics*
> *and Angie is like your new favorite*
> *person and Michael died and what*
> *do I even SAY?*

I tell Jenny,
You just say, I'm sorry.
The worst thing happened
and it sucks.
That's all.
I know you can't fix it.
No one can.

Jenny says,
I'm sorry,
the worst thing happened to you
and it sucks. So hard.

MY EYES FILL WITH TEARS

Mostly from happiness.
She apologized!
She cares about me.

I say,

Love you, Jenny.

    Love you, Kelly.
    For real.

We hang up.

I know I need to
finish social studies.

But I feel so antsy.

Because I want to tell
someone *else* the news.

I made the team!
Jenny and I made up!

And then I realize
the person I want to tell
is Michael.

WHY NOT?

I think about what
Angie told me,
about writing letters
to her dad.

And I figure,

why not?

Dear Michael,

I miss you.

I hope you know how much I miss you.
It's not the same without you.

But I'm trying to
keep this letter happy
because I have the most
awesome news.

I MADE THE TEAM!!!

I didn't think I would
because there were finalists
and only one spot left.
It was stressful
to the max,
Michael.
It really was.

I had no one to talk to
and Todd was being such a total
waste of space.

He got engaged!
To TRACY.
Can you believe it?

And maybe I started dating someone?
Brandon.
He's such a good listener!
And cute, of course.

I'm super sad you'll never meet him.

Maybe we'll go on an
"official" double date
with Jenny and her boyfriend, Ryan.

OH, and Jenny and I got in a huge fight
and she actually apologized!

I SET MY PEN DOWN

and for a moment,
it's almost like he's here.

Like maybe Michael can hear me?

I feel hopeful.

I've had an awesome day.

And it breaks my heart
Michael isn't here.

It's felt so lonely,
being alone with my
memories of him.

I wanted to talk to my family.
And I've realized I can't, not really.

But I've found a safe way
to remember him.

And that's progress.

JENNY WON'T STOP MESSING

with my bangs.

Oh my god, Jenny.
They look fine!

> *Fine isn't good enough.*
> *We're going for totally awesome!*

I think my bangs do
look totally awesome.
But I'm happy to have Jenny back.
I missed her.

I don't think Brandon cares this much
about my bangs, Jenny.

> *I care this much about bangs.*
> *This is our first official double date*
> *and it's going to be totally tubular!*

I'M KIND OF NERVOUS

but also excited . . .

but mostly nervous.

We meet the boys at the pier.
Brandon and I smile at each other.
Jenny runs up to Ryan and hugs him.
Like she's
going to knock him over.

Oh my God, this is so epic!

She spins around,

I love the pier at sunset!

She's right. It's super pretty.

BUT WHAT DO I SAY

on a *date*?

I feel weird.

Jenny and Ryan are holding hands
and leading the way.

She's whispering in his ear
and giggling.

Brandon and I are walking
together, silently.

And then he asks,

So what happened?
Did you make the team?

I can't believe I didn't tell him.

Yes! I did!
I can't believe it.

And then he hugs me.
And I don't want him to let go.

AFTER DINNER WE STAND

at the end of the pier and look out
into the night.

Brandon listens to me
ramble on about
gymnastics and Angie
and Mary Lou Retton—

I'm geeking out.

But he doesn't seem to mind.

We have our first meet next Saturday,
it's super—

BRANDON TAKES MY HAND

and I forget what I was saying.

I just look down at our hands.

Whatever the opposite
of being totally chill is,
that's me right now.

Unchill.
The Unchillest.

I look up at Brandon,
and he just smiles
at me.

He doesn't think
I'm weird.

He just squeezes my hand
and tells me
to keep talking.

WHEN I GET HOME

I'm walking on air.
I'm happy.

My parents sit silently
in front of the TV
watching some stupid movie.

My dad is asleep,
his chin on his chest.

I give my mom a kiss
on the top of her head
and head up to my room.

I WRITE TO MICHAEL

about Brandon.

I try hard not to feel bad
about living my life
when Michael doesn't get to anymore.

It's not fair.
It never will be.

And I know it might sound strange,
but I feel like Michael is
somewhere and

he's really happy for me.

COACH CAROL FRENCH BRAIDS

my hair so tight, it almost feels
like she's ripping my hair
out of my head.

I know better than to complain.

She wraps a rubber band
around the end
and sprays so much hairspray
that I feel like
I might start coughing.

I HOLD MY BREATH

until she's finished.
And once she is, I smile
big and say,

Thank you!

You're welcome, Kelly.
Good luck.

I'll take it.

I need all the luck I can get.

ANGIE IS FLAWLESS

and her scores reflect that.

It's great for the team.
It looks like we should
easily win the meet.

Coach Gary paces back and forth.
Making sure we're ready.

He pats me on the back before
my bar routine,
and says,

You got this, Kelly.

I CHALK UP

Then I clap my hands together
and salute the judges.

I mount the bars and my routine
is going well.

My rhythm is good,
I'm hitting my handstands,
my toes are pointed.

I release the high bar
to move down to the low bar—

but my grip isn't perfect.

I'M SLIPPING!

But then—

in a split second,
I move my grip
without losing
my rhythm.

And then I dismount.
And I stick the landing.

I am so stoked.

I could have fallen
and ruined my routine.

But I'm strong enough now
to know how to recover.

ANGIE TAKES FIRST

in the all-around
and our team wins first.

The whole team gets up
on the podium,
holding our first place
blue ribbons,

hugging each other and smiling.

I SQUEEZE ANGIE

and scream,

First place!
I'm so happy for you!

And I am.

I'm bummed I didn't place in
all-arounds.
But there are a bunch more
meets this season.

And I have a really good feeling.

Things are looking up.

MOM, DAD, AND TODD

take me out for dinner
to celebrate my first meet.

We're so proud of you, Kelly!

My mom gushes.

Way to go, Kelly,
Todd agrees.

And I think he actually
means it.
He hasn't been as harsh lately,
now that he's in love.

My dad doesn't say much,
but he smiles and nods.

I like to imagine that means
he's proud too.

TODD GIVES ME A HUG

and pats me on the back.

I think he's trying.
And I'm going to try too.

I know
Michael's death changed us.

My parents aren't the same.
Todd isn't who he used to be.
And neither am I.

I'm starting to realize
that we will never turn back
into the people we were.

Instead, we need to figure out
how to live as the people
we are now.

WHEN I GET HOME

I head to my room,
pull out my journal,
and start writing to Michael.

He's not the same either.
But he's still here with me.
He matters to me.
And I know he always will.

THE PHONE RINGS

I figure it's Jenny,
but it's Angie,
which is such a rad surprise.

She wants to plan a sleepover
at her house
with her best friend from school
and me,
her best friend from the gym.

WE HANG UP

and I pick up my pen,
writing down every detail
of the meet.

I'm so excited to tell Michael:

We won first place!

I almost lost my grip,
but didn't!

I wasn't jealous of Angie
but happy for her!

I can feel the smile spreading
across my face as I
think of all the things and
people who make
my life awesome.

ON MONDAY

We're back at practice,
and there's no place
I'd rather be.

I'm working on my new vault!

Round off
back handspring layout.

I'm flying!
I feel so powerful.
I love it.

Angie hollers after my first attempt,

Yes, Kelly!
Perfect 10!

I KNOW

I'm not perfect
yet.

And maybe that's
an impossible goal.

But in honor of Michael—

I'm going to have
so much fun
getting there.

WANT TO KEEP READING?

If you liked this book, check out another book from West 44 Books:
CATCH ME IF I FALL
BY CLAUDIA RECINOS SELDEEN

ISBN: 9781978597037

BALANCING ACT

Hang
on
tight!

When I'm on a trapeze,
I defy gravity.

I'm a leaf
caught in a summer storm.
Twisting.
Spinning.

But there's always that voice
in the back of my mind,
whispering:

Hang
on
tight.

Don't
let
go.

Falling is not an option.

DANCE TRAPEZE

When I tell people
I'm a
trapeze artist,
their eyes
light up
like stars.

I know
they're thinking about
flying
            trapeze.
About acrobats
w h i z z i n g
through the air.

But
dance
            trapeze
is
different.

There's no
swinging.
No catching.
No letting go.

A
dance
            trapeze
doesn't
tick tock
back and forth.

A
dance
          trapeze
spins
in tight circles.

It twirls
and turns.

If you don't hold on,
it will
spin
you
right
off.

NOODLE

After every trapeze class,
I lie on my bedroom floor
and let the bruises
bloom.

That's what
no one tells you
about trapeze.

The bar is made of metal.
The ropes can slip
and burn.

When my mom
calls me for dinner,
I trudge
down
the
stairs
on wobbly legs.

If AnnMarie were here,
she'd call me a
noodle.

She'd flop her arms
like boiled spaghetti
and make me
laugh.
She can
always
make
me
laugh.

But AnnMarie
isn't here.

My best friend
can't come over
on trapeze days.

ABOUT THE AUTHOR

Alyson Shelton is an award-winning screenwriter and essayist. Her writing is widely published at outlets including *The New York Times, Ms.*, and T*he Rumpus.* She's anthologized in *No Contact: Writers on Estrangement, Root Cause: Stories of Health, Harm and Reclaiming Our Humanity, Comics Lit: Vol. 1, Spell Check: Lessons Learned from Screwing Up Words* and *The Loss of a Lifetime: Grieving Siblings Share Stories of Love, Loss, and Hope* (Contributor and Co-Editor). She's best known for her Instagram Live series inspired by George Ella Lyon's poem, *Where I'm From*, where she's hosted over 250 writers. This is her first book for teen readers.